For my favorite travel agent, Sue Beechey —S. M.

I would like to dedicate the illustrations in this book
to my dearest friend Liz. —D. T.

ACKNOWLEDGMENTS

The author would like to thank the following people for sharing their enthusiasm and expertise: Harry Rutstein, Founder of the Marco Polo Foundation; and Dr. Peter Jackson of the Keele University Department of Biology, Keele, United Kingdom.

As always a special thank you to Skip Jeffery for his help and support through the creative process.

Book design by Katie Jennings.
Typeset in Dorovar and New Renaissance.
The illustrations in this book were
rendered in mixed media.
Manufactured in China.

10 9 8 7 6 5 4 3 2 1

Chronicle Books LLC
680 Second Street
San Francisco, California 94107

www.chroniclekids.com

Library of Congress Cataloging-in-Publication-Data
Markle, Sandra.
Animals Marco Polo saw : an adventure on the Silk Road /
by Sandra Markle ; illustrator, Daniela Terrazzini.
p. cm.
ISBN 978-0-8118-5051-3
1. Polo, Marco, 1254–1323?—Travel—Juvenile literature.
2. Explorers—Italy—Biography—Juvenile literature.
3. Voyages and travels—Juvenile literature. 4. Travel,
Medieval—Juvenile literature. 5. Asia—Description and
travel—Juvenile literature. 6. Animals—Asia—Juvenile
literature. I. Terrazzini, Daniela, ill. II. Title.
G370.P9M38 2009
591.9509'022—dc22
2007053057

ANIMALS *Marco Polo* SAW

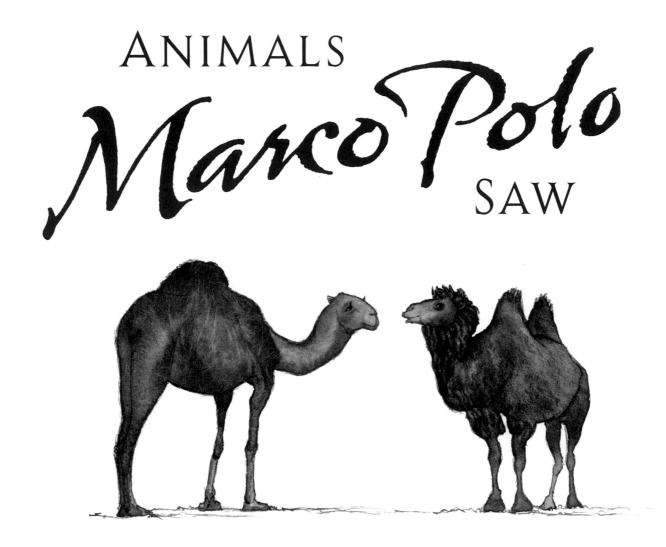

AN ADVENTURE ON THE SILK ROAD

By SANDRA MARKLE · Illustrated by DANIELA JAGLENKA TERRAZZINI

chronicle books · san francisco

NOTE TO PARENTS AND TEACHERS

The books in the Explorers series take young readers back in time to share explorations that had a major impact on people's view of the world. Kids will investigate why and how the explorers made their journeys and learn about animals they discovered along the way. They'll find out how some animals affected the outcome of the journey: helping explorers find their way, causing key events to happen, or helping the explorers survive. Young readers will also learn that, because of the explorers' journeys, animals were introduced to places they'd never lived before, sometimes with dramatic results.

The Explorers series helps students develop the following key concepts:

From the National Council for the Social Studies:
Human beings seek to understand their historical roots and to locate themselves in time. Such understanding involves knowing what things were like in the past and how things change and develop. Students also learn to draw on their knowledge of history to make informed choices and decisions in the present.

From the National Academy of Sciences:
Making sense of the way organisms live in their environments will develop an understanding of the diversity of life and how all living organisms depend on the living and nonliving environment for survival.

Contents

The First Travel Guide

Imagine not knowing what an entire part of the world is like, and not being able to easily do research to find out. The idea may seem strange, since today nearly every part of the world has been explored and photos of most places are available in books, on television, and on the Internet. But in explorer Marco Polo's time, most people didn't travel far from home. Those who did couldn't easily share what they discovered with large numbers of people. The printing press hadn't yet been invented, so books had to be written by hand. And since Marco lived long before the invention of automobiles, airplanes, trucks, and trains, there was no easy way to distribute books far and wide.

After spending years traveling the world, Marco told people about his adventures. His stories were written down, and they became the world's very first travel guide. What is today called *The Travels of Marco Polo* describes his travels to Mongolia and the Far East, a part of the world that includes China, Japan, Thailand, and the other countries of East Asia. Many people in Europe thought the Far East was exotic and mysterious, and they were curious about his journey. But why did he go in the first place? And what did he discover along the way? You may be surprised to learn about the animals he encountered, some of which played a key part in his journey.

Dreams of Adventure

Marco Polo was born in Italy on September 15, 1254. He was from a family of merchants who sold very popular, but expensive, silks and spices from the Far East. These goods had to be carried through several countries along a route known as the Silk Road. One reason silks and spices were so expensive was that they came from so far away.

Marco was only a little boy in 1260 when his father, Niccolò, and uncle Maffeo left on a buying trip to Cathay (KATH-ay), now called China. By the time they returned, Marco was 15. His mother had died, and he was living with relatives. Marco's father shared many fascinating stories of the faraway places he had visited during the many years he was gone.

COSTLY WORMS

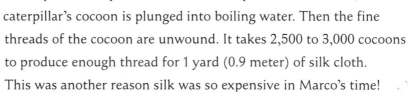

In the 1200s, Europeans believed silk cloth was made from plants. But silk is made from threads produced by a kind of moth caterpillar. To make silk, the caterpillar's cocoon is plunged into boiling water. Then the fine threads of the cocoon are unwound. It takes 2,500 to 3,000 cocoons to produce enough thread for 1 yard (0.9 meter) of silk cloth. This was another reason silk was so expensive in Marco's time!

On a Mission for Kublai Khan

Niccolò and Maffeo hadn't planned to stay away as long or to travel as far as they did. Their plans to return to Venice were disrupted by a war that broke out and blocked their route. So they changed course and ended up in Bukhara, Uzbekistan (OOZ-beck-ih-stan), where they stayed for almost three years. While in Bukhara, the Polos were invited to visit Kublai Khan (KOO-bluh KHAN), the ruler of Cathay.

Kublai Khan was very curious about Europe and fascinated by the Polos' life there. He was particularly interested in their descriptions of Christianity and wanted to learn more. He sent the Polo brothers back to Europe with a request for the Catholic Pope. The Khan asked for a hundred priests to teach his people about Christianity. The Khan also asked the Polo brothers to bring him holy oil from the lamp at Jesus' tomb in Jerusalem (juh-ROO-suh-lum).

PASSPORT INCLUDES HORSES
Kublai Khan gave the Polo brothers a golden tablet—a passport that meant they could travel safely throughout the land he controlled. It also meant they could stop anywhere within the Khan's empire for free food and lodging and fresh horses.

Because Kublai Khan was a powerful ruler and an important trade partner, the Polo brothers decided to complete the mission he had given them. They returned to Europe, and by the time they gathered everything they needed to return to Cathay, Marco was 17. He was eager to go along for the adventure. Niccolò decided this was a good idea, a chance for Marco to learn the family business.

First, the Polos traveled to Rome to ask the Pope to send the one hundred priests the Khan had requested. The Pope agreed to send only two friars. The Polos were disappointed, but there was nothing they could do. The Polos and the two friars went to Jerusalem to collect holy oil for the Khan. They were about to leave Jerusalem for Cathay when a war broke out along their travel route. Frightened, the friars fled, but the Polos decided to go on.

NIGHT LIFE

Around Jerusalem, Marco probably saw animals he had never seen before—especially at night. He may have seen foxlike jackals. These animals are scavengers. Their keen sense of smell lets them detect odors as much as a half mile (0.8 kilometer) away. And Marco may have seen them cleaning up the city's garbage.

The Adventure Begins

The Polos purchased horses to ride and carry their supplies. They joined a caravan and set off, heading back to Kublai Khan's court. Everywhere Marco went he was amazed by what he saw. The land looked very different from Venice. Many of the animals Marco saw along the way were unfamiliar, too. While traveling through Turkey, Marco saw boars, mountain goats, and bears. When they reached Lake Van, the largest lake in Turkey, the caravan camped on its shore. Marco was surprised to discover the water was brackish, meaning it was salty but not as salty as seawater. The only fish capable of living in the lake was a kind of mullet.

In Armenia, Marco slept at the foot of snow-capped Mount Ararat. He knew of this mountain from the Bible. Mount Ararat was reported to be the resting place of Noah's ark.

RARE CAT

Marco may have seen a rare kind of cat around Lake Van. Called a Van cat, it is a native of the lake area. Unlike most cats, Van cats are good swimmers. Many also have two differently colored eyes: one blue and one green.

Attacked!

A little farther on, the Polos' caravan crossed a dry plain. Strong winds whipped up clouds of dust. Suddenly, a band of men appeared amid the swirling dust and attacked the caravan. Marco had heard about fierce tribesmen who surprised their victims in dust storms. When they attacked the Polos' caravan, Marco rode away as fast as his horse could run. Several of the tribesmen chased after him, but Marco escaped into a walled village. Luckily, Niccolò and Maffeo also escaped, but the tribesmen stole some of the caravan's goods and killed some of the travelers. Marco began to understand that the world was home to different groups of people with very different ways of living.

ZEBU OXEN

When the caravan crossed into Persia (today's Iran), Marco saw oxen with humps on their backs. These were probably zebu oxen. Since ancient times, people have used these strong oxen to haul carts and pull plows.

When he visited the city of Baku on the Caspian Sea, Marco saw something else that surprised him. It was a fountain bubbling out of the ground, but its liquid was thick and black. The liquid was oil. Marco said there was so much of it that a hundred ships might be filled with it at one time. He also saw oil seeping out onto the ground and people scooping it up. Oil was already valued in Marco Polo's time. However, then it was burned in lamps and used to treat skin rashes.

OIL!

In Marco Polo's time, no one knew oil was the remains of ancient animals. Millions of years earlier, Earth's seas and swamps were soup-thick with tiny animals, algae, and bacteria. As these died, their remains settled to the bottom and were covered with layers of mud. Over millions of years, more layers of mud piled up. Gradually the pressure of the overlying layers turned the remains into oil.

Turning Point

The Polos left the caravan in Hormuz (HOR-muz), a port city along a river that leads into the Persian Gulf. Niccolò and Maffeo thought sailing to China would be easier than trekking overland, as they had done before.

While his father and uncle tried to secure passage on a boat, Marco explored Hormuz. He was impressed by the beauty of this hot, tropical place. Flocks of colorful parrots flew overhead. He also spotted ducks, egrets, pelicans, and herons in the river and along its shore. During the hot part of the day, Marco saw lots of people in the river and may have joined them. It was a good way to escape the nearly unbearable heat.

ANIMAL GIANTS

While exploring Hormuz, Marco stopped in the market. There he saw elephant tusks for sale. He probably also saw these giant animals at work and cooling off in the river. Elephants are the largest land animals in Asia. Since ancient times, they have been used for big jobs, such as moving heavy logs.

Follow the Silk Road

When Niccolò and Maffeo discovered that the hulls of boats available in Hormuz were laced together—not nailed, like those of European ships—they worried the boats might break apart in a storm. So together with Marco, they joined another caravan and continued along the Silk Road. When they passed the ruins of an ancient city, Marco saw lions for the first time. He was impressed. Some people on the caravan may have talked about hunting the lions. Others were probably worried the lions might attack when the caravan stopped for the night.

NO MORE ROAR

The lions Marco saw were Persian lions. Persian lions looked a lot like African lions but had a thicker coat. Male Persian lions also had a shorter mane than male African lions. Hunting these lions was once such a popular sport that Persian lions are now extinct, meaning none are alive today.

Time-Out

Marco had not felt well since he left Hormuz, and he eventually became too ill to go on. The Polos left the caravan and stopped at a village in Badakhshan (BAH-da-ki-shan), known as Tajikistan (TAH-ji-ki-stan) today. Marco soon felt better, but the Polos stayed for about a year to let him fully recover. Once he was strong enough to go outdoors, Marco got to know the local people. He was impressed by how well the men hunted with bows and arrows. They kept everyone supplied with plenty of meat to eat and skins for making clothes. Because the village was high in the mountains, where winters are cold, the Polos probably bought or traded for fur coats.

SNOW CAT

Marco may have seen people wearing coats made of snow leopard fur. This cat's thick, soft fur has been valued for clothing since ancient times, but snow leopards live high in the mountains and are not easy to hunt. They can run fast and leap over 40 feet (about 12 meters) in one bound.

PRICKLY GAME

Marco often saw the hunters bring home porcupines for dinner. For defense, they have special stiff guard hairs called quills. But these cannot protect the porcupines from a hunter's arrow.

To the Roof of the World

When the Polos set off again, they joined another caravan. Then they trekked across a rugged mountain range called the Pamirs (PUH-mirz). The mountains are so high that clouds often hide their peaks. At one point, the caravan was so high up that Marco stopped seeing birds. No wonder the local people called the Pamirs the "roof of the world"! Heading down the other side of the mountains, Marco saw birds again, and an amazing, unfamiliar kind of sheep with the biggest horns he had ever seen. The males' horns were so long that they curled into big corkscrews.

YAK IT UP THE MOUNTAIN

Cousins of cattle, yaks were the trucks of the mountain caravans. Their thick coats kept them warm in places too cold for many other animals. And they could carry heavy loads in places too high for most other pack animals to work. Their waste was fuel for campfires in places too high for travelers to find firewood. People rode the yaks, too. A yak saddle was like a legless wooden chair. Imagine how uncomfortable it was!

MARCO'S SHEEP

The mountain sheep that impressed Marco are today named Marco Polo sheep *(Ovis poli)* in his honor. The males use their big horns to battle for mates. Some have horns that, if uncurled, would be as long as 5 feet (1.5 meters).

Across the Desert of No Return

Once the caravan reached the city of Kashgar (KASH-gar) at the foot of the mountains, the Polos were in Cathay. But they still had a long way to go to reach Kublai Khan. Just ahead were two deserts: the Gobi (GOH-bee) and the Taklimakan (TAH-kluh-MUH-kan). The Gobi is Asia's largest desert. The Taklimakan is Asia's driest, hottest desert. It is such a harsh environment its name means "desert of no return." Although it is at the edge of the desert, Kashgar had water and beautiful gardens, which Marco enjoyed. To prepare for the next part of their journey, the Polos traded for camels and purchased the supplies they would need. Then they set off again. At first, the caravan trekked from one oasis to the next. Then the caravan traveled through the desert for more than thirty days.

ONE HUMP OR TWO?

There are two kinds of camels: Arabian, also called Dromedary, and Bactrian (BAK-tree-uhn). Arabian camels have just one hump. Bactrian have two.

Both kinds of camels are suited for hauling goods across deserts. Their wide footpads keep them from sinking into the sand. Their long eyelashes keep blowing sand out of their eyes. And camels can go several weeks without drinking water.

Across a Sea of Grass

Finally, the caravan left the desert behind. Then they traveled across a region called the Mongolian steppes (STEPZ), which look like a sea of grass stretching to the horizon. Once again, Marco encountered people with a very different way of life from his own: the Mongolians. They were nomads, people who moved when their animals needed fresh pasture. They lived in round felt-covered tents called gers (GAREZ), also known as yurts (YURTZ). They counted on their yaks, sheep, and goats for meat, milk, and wool for clothing. But the animals that the Mongolians valued most were their horses.

ALL THE KHAN'S HORSES

Kublai Khan's ancestors were Mongolians, so he, too, valued horses. And his favorites were pure white horses. He believed they were lucky. He also liked to drink kumiss (kim-iz), fermented mare's milk.

The Mongolians were amazing horsemen. The children were taught to ride when they were only three. By five, they could shoot bows and arrows while riding. No wonder Mongol archers could hit a target from the back of a galloping horse! Mongol armies were famous for riding long distances without stopping. On horseback they conquered the huge Mongol Empire, which extended from eastern Europe through Asia. The empire remained in power from about the early thirteenth century through most of the fourteenth century. Different Mongol rulers governed different sections of the empire. Kublai Khan controlled a large area, including Cathay.

HORSE POST

Marco was impressed with the Mongolian postal system. Mail was divided into classes depending on how fast it needed to be delivered. Runners on foot delivered second-class mail. Riders on horseback delivered first-class mail. The mail was passed from one rider to another at special post stops. A single rider who changed horses along the way delivered the Khan's personal mail.

Visiting the Great Khan

In 1274, the Polos' journey neared its end. When they were still about 300 miles (482 kilometers) away from the capital city of Cambuluc (KAM-bu-luk, now Beijing), Kublai Khan had guards meet them and escort them to his vacation home at Changde (CHUNG-duh).

Marco was amazed—again. Of all the places he had seen so far, this was the most fantastic. The Khan's vacation home was a huge palace of marble and gold. Beautiful parks surrounded it and stretched out farther than he could see. To remind the Khan of his Mongolian roots, there was also a ger, but this one was big enough for a crowd. And it was made of gold-covered wood and lion skins.

HUNTING CAT

Kublai Khan loved to go hunting in his parks. He sometimes hunted with a tame leopard riding on his horse. When the Khan spotted a deer, he turned the leopard loose and watched it chase down the deer.

Going Home

For 17 years, the Polos worked for the Great Khan. Marco, by then an adult, impressed the Khan with his good observations and ability to quickly learn different languages. The Khan sent Marco around Cathay and to Burma and India as his official representative to report on all that was going on in those parts of his empire. Niccolò and Maffeo helped the Khan continue his efforts to expand his empire. They designed and supervised construction of special weapons, such as catapults and towers for scaling walls.

The Polos were not unhappy with their work, and they lived very well. Still, they wanted to go back to their homeland and family. They repeatedly asked to leave, but the Khan repeatedly refused to let them. Then a Mongol princess was promised in marriage to the Khan's grand-nephew in Persia. The Khan ordered the Polos to join a huge group that would escort her safely to her wedding. At last they had a chance to escape the Khan's court!

This time the Polos traveled by sea rather than overland. Storms sank many of the ships in their fleet. Enemies attacked and killed many of the soldiers and servants in their party. But the Polos and the princess survived. Once they had delivered her as promised, they headed home. Along the way, the Polos were attacked and robbed by bandits, but they managed to escape unharmed. In 1295, they finally returned to Venice. After all they had been through, their clothes were rags, but they held a surprise. The Polos had sewn jewels into the seams of their coats—enough to make their whole family rich!

WHALE OF A TALE
While at sea, Marco probably saw gray whales. These sea giants grow to be as much as 49 feet (15 meters) long. But they eat mainly tiny animals. They get this food by opening their mouths and swimming. This pushes the water through comblike filters that strain out food for the whale to swallow.

A World Changed Forever

A few years later, in 1298, there was a battle between the towns of Venice and Genoa (JE-nuh-wuh), Italy. Marco fought in this battle and was captured. While in prison, he shared stories of his travels with his fellow captives. His stories were so interesting that another prisoner wrote them down and called the collection *The Description of the World*. Soon other people were copying this book and passing it around. The printing press had not yet been invented, so every copy had to be handwritten. But the book was

very popular, and many people made copies. It was even translated into different European languages. After a while, much of Europe was talking about Marco Polo's travels.

Suddenly, people wanted to know more about the world. Many European countries sent people out to explore. New interactions between the West and the East had begun. For better and for worse, they would change the world forever.

Map of
Marco Polo's Travels

Venice

ITALY

Black Sea

CASPIAN
SEA

Baku

UZBEKISTAN

MONGOLIAN
STEPPES

TURKEY

ARMENIA

Mt. Ararat

IRAN

TAJIKISTAN

Kashgar

GOBI
DESERT

ISRAEL
Jerusalem

Hormuz

Pamirs Mountain Range

CHINA

PERSIAN
GULF

TAKLIMAKAN
DESERT

INDIA

BURMA

THAILAND

Glossary

caravan [KAAR-uh-van]   a group of travelers crossing a desert or other harsh environment together

empire [EM-piir]   the name given to an area made up of many nations joined together under one ruler, usually by being conquered

ger [GARE]   the name the Mongolian nomads on the steppes gave to their tent homes, constructed of felt stretched over a wooden frame

Khan [KHAN]   the Mongol name meaning "ruler"

Mongols [MAHNG-gulz]   the nomads who lived on the Mongolian steppes. They were such great horsemen and fighters that they conquered a vast empire for Genghis Khan. Later, this was expanded and ruled by his grandson Kublai Khan.

nomads [NOH-madz]   people who move from place to place in search of food and water for themselves and their herds of animals

silk [SILK]   a natural fiber produced when the caterpillar of the silk moth spins a cocoon

Silk Road [SILK ROHD]   the name given to a series of routes used by caravans heading from the Far East to the West, carrying goods such as spices, jade, gold, ivory, and silk

spice [SPIIS]   any of a number of vegetable products, such as pepper, used to flavor food

steppes [STEPZ]   the name given to the large grasslands of Central Asia and the Far East

FOR MORE INFORMATION

To learn more about Marco Polo and the animals and places he saw during his journey, check out these books and Web sites.

Books:

Marco Polo for Kids, by Janise Herbert (Chicago Review Press, 2001) In addition to discovering the history of Marco Polo's travels, you can share activities and learn Turkish, Persian, Mongol, Hindi, and Chinese words from the cultures he encountered.

The World in the Time of Marco Polo, by Fiona MacDonald (Dillon Press, 1997) Discover what was happening in the world at the time Marco Polo made his amazing journey.

Video:

Biography: Marco Polo (A&E Entertainment, 2000).
Follow Marco Polo's epic journey while discovering what experts have learned about his personal life.

Web sites:

The Travels of Marco Polo
website.lineone.net/~mcrouch/marcopolo/marcopolo.htm
Dig deeper into Marco Polo's travels and learn about the people he met and what the world was like in his time. Don't miss the links that let you explore even further.

Index